AVATAR
THE LAST AIRBENDER.

SOKKA,
the Sword Master

adapted by Sherry Gerstein
based on the screenplay by Tim Hedrick
illustrated by Patrick Spaziante

Ready-to-Read

Simon Spotlight
New York   London   Toronto   Sydney

Based on the TV series *Nickelodeon Avatar: The Last Airbender*™ as seen on Nickelodeon®

SIMON SPOTLIGHT
An imprint of Simon & Schuster Children's Publishing Division
1230 Avenue of the Americas, New York, New York 10020
© 2008 Viacom International Inc. All rights reserved. NICKELODEON, *Nickelodeon Avatar: The Last Airbender*, and all related titles, logos, and characters are trademarks of Viacom International Inc.
SIMON SPOTLIGHT, READY-TO-READ, and colophon are registered trademarks of Simon & Schuster, Inc.
Manufactured in the United States of America
First Edition
2 4 6 8 10 9 7 5 3 1
Library of Congress Cataloging-in-Publication Data
Gerstein, Sherry.
Sokka, the sword master / adapted by Sherry Gerstein ; based on the screenplay by Tim Hedrick ; illustrated by Patrick Spaziante. —1st ed.
p. cm. — (Ready-to-read)
"Based on the TV series Nickelodeon Avatar: The Last Airbender as seen on Nickelodeon."
ISBN-13: 978-1-4169-5491-0
ISBN-10: 1-4169-5491-0
I. Hedrick, Tim. II. Spaziante, Patrick. III. Title.
PZ7.G32515Sok 2008
2007023700

CHAPTER 1

Aang and his friends were in the Fire Nation. One night a fiery meteorite crashed near a village. Aang, Toph, and Katara flew over on Appa to help. Together they bended air, earth, and water to put out the fire.

Sokka stayed behind. "What do I do?" he asked Aang.

"Keep an eye on Momo," Aang replied.

Sokka fumed. "What am I—a lemur-sitter?!"

The next day Toph had one complaint. "The worst thing about being in disguise is no more hero worship," she said.

"Boo-hoo! Poor heroes!" sneered Sokka. The others looked at him, puzzled.

"All you guys can do this awesome bending stuff," Sokka explained. "Not me. I can't do anything! I'm just the guy in the group who's regular."

"We don't see you that way," Katara told her brother. "And I know what will cheer you up."

"Shopping!" exclaimed Sokka. He looked around the Fire Nation weapons shop.

Sokka tried out weapons one by one: spears, maces, and nunchakus. Then he saw the most beautiful sword ever!

"That was made by Master Piandao, who lives just down the road," the shopkeeper said.

Aang had an idea. "We've all had masters helping us," he told Sokka. "Maybe you can study with Piandao."

"A master sword fighter," said Sokka. "I'll do it!"

CHAPTER 2

Sokka pounded on the door to Piandao's house. The door opened, and a servant peered down at Sokka.

"I'm here to train with the master," Sokka said as he bowed respectfully.

"The master turns nearly everyone away," the servant warned. "What have you brought to show your worth?"

Sokka shook his head. He had nothing. The servant snorted, but led him into the house.

Sokka bowed as he greeted Piandao. "Master, my name is Sokka," he said. "I've come to learn the way of the sword."

"Sokka is an unusual name," Piandao said.

Sokka had to think of a quick reply. "Uh, it's pretty normal where I'm from . . . the Fire Nation colonies."

"And you think you deserve to learn from me?" Piandao asked.

Sokka dropped to his knees. "I've got a lot to learn," he said. "I don't know if I am worthy."

Piandao was impressed with Sokka's humble spirit. "Let's find out if you are worthy together."

CHAPTER 3

Piandao and Sokka were in the garden. The master had a sword in his hand and lunged forward. "Think of your sword as a really sharp, extra-long arm," Piandao said.

He demonstrated proper sword stance and showed Sokka how to position his fingers for balance. "When you truly master the sword, you are like a bender with his element. You feel its energy as it responds to you."

Piandao led his pupil to a table with art supplies. He handed Sokka a brush. "A warrior uses many skills to keep his mind sharp. You stamp your identity on the paper when you write your name," explained the master. "A good warrior must do the same thing in battle."

Sokka tapped his cheek with his brush as he thought.

"You are getting ink on your face," said Piandao, which gave Sokka an idea. He swept ink across his face and then put his head down, and rolled his face across the paper. An inky Sokka face print appeared!

Piandao stared at it without saying a word.

It was time for Sokka to learn to spar. Using wooden practice swords, he sparred with Fat, Piandao's servant. Sokka lunged forward many times. And each time Fat blocked the thrust and easily flicked away Sokka's sword.

Sokka's second sparring session with Fat went better. He was starting to think of a sword as an extended arm.

"Sokka!" Piandao barked. Sokka turned to look at his master. And Fat chose that moment to knock him down.

"Concentrate!" scolded the master. Sokka could only nod his head.

For the next lesson, Piandao blindfolded Sokka. "Landscape painting teaches a warrior to hold the lay of the land in his mind," Piandao said. "You'll only have an instant to take everything in during battle."

Then he removed the blindfold. Sokka found himself gazing at a river with mountains in the background. The master spun him around to face an easel and some paints.

"Paint! And no peeking!" commanded Piandao.

Sokka painted for a while. Then he shouted, "I'm finished!"

"You put in a rainbow," Piandao noted.

"Is that okay?" Sokka asked, a little worried.

The master looked at his pupil thoughtfully.

"Rock gardening teaches a warrior to use his surroundings to his advantage," Piandao said as they stood in the rock garden.

Sokka was sure of himself as he moved rocks around. He took some soft, springy moss and then . . . it was done.

Piandao stared at his pupil, and was amused. Sokka was proving to be quite an unusual student!

Sokka's third sparring session was the best yet. He had full control of his sword now. With a quick block and a thrust, Fat was disarmed. Then, in the blink of an eye, Sokka was on his back—again! Fat grinned down at him. In his hand was Sokka's own sword!

At the end of the day Sokka knelt before Piandao. "You've had a good day," Piandao told him.

Sokka was surprised. "I have? But I messed up every single thing."

Piandao nodded. "True, but you messed them up in a special way. You are ready to make your own sword." He led Sokka into his workshop. Showing him many types of steel bars, the master said, "You will have to trust the steel with your life, so choose carefully."

Sokka looked at the steel bars, then asked, "Would it be all right if I brought in some material for my sword?"

Piandao smiled. "I wouldn't have it any other way."

CHAPTER 4

"Sokka's coming!" With Toph's finely tuned senses, the blind Earthbender could hear Sokka's footsteps long before he appeared.

"We missed you!" Katara cried when she saw her brother.

Sokka took them to the meteorite crater, where they all looked down at the large space

rock. "Can you help me move that?" he asked.

A short while later, the four friends arrived at Piandao's house with the rock.

"My friends helped me bring this rock here," Sokka explained. "Can we make a sword out of a meteorite?"

"We'll make a sword unlike any other in the world," Piandao replied.

21

Piandao coached as Sokka worked. They broke off bits of the rock and melted it down. Piandao poured the liquid metal into a mold, and then showed Sokka how to hammer it into shape. Using a grinding wheel, Sokka sharpened the blade's edges. He fitted the blade into a handle. What had once been a rock was now a thing of beauty.

Sokka knelt before his master once more.

"Sokka," Piandao began, "you are creative, intelligent, and able to think on your feet. These are what make a great swordsman."

He presented Sokka with the sword. "You once told me that you didn't know if you were worthy," the master added. "I say you are more worthy than any man I have ever trained."

Sokka hung his head. "Master, I'm not from the Fire Nation. I lied so you would show me the way of the sword. I'm sorry."

Suddenly Piandao trembled with rage. "I'm sorry too," he growled as he drew his sword.

The others sprang to Sokka's defense, but he waved them away. "This is my fight," Sokka told them. And he drew his own sword.

CHAPTER 5

The two combatants circled each other. Suddenly Piandao lunged forward. The master had body weight and experience on his side. Sokka, however, was more agile. He managed to block the thrust and climb up some stairs.

"Good use of terrain, fighting from the high ground," called the master.

Sokka narrowed his eyes. Why was Piandao praising him?

Piandao bore down on him, but Sokka warded him off, pushing off from a wall.

"Very smart, using your superior agility over an older opponent," Piandao remarked.

Sokka ran through a thicket of bamboo, slicing with every stride. Bamboo poles fell behind him, blocking Piandao's path.

Piandao knocked the poles aside with his sword. "Yes!" he cried. "Make your surroundings work for you!"

Sokka scrambled to get away from the master, and almost lost his footing. As he skidded, he came up with an idea. Sokka grabbed a handful of dirt and gravel, and threw it in Piandao's face.

Piandao groaned, yet still praised Sokka. "Very resourceful!" he said as he spat out the dirt.

With Piandao blinded, Sokka tried to tiptoe past him, but he stepped on a twig. And the master zeroed in on the sound.

Sokka, however, was finally out of tricks.
Piandao moved in quickly and knocked away
his sword. Sokka tumbled to the ground,
fearing the worst.

Instead, Piandao put away his sword. The
fight was over! The master faced Aang,
Katara, and Toph, who were ready for battle.
Then he shocked everyone.

"I'm too old to be fighting the Avatar,"
Piandao said.

"How did you know?" asked Aang.

"Oh, I've been around for a while," the
master replied. "I knew all along that Sokka
was from the Water Tribe." Then he told
Sokka, "You need a better Fire Nation cover
name. Try Lee. There are a million Lees."

"The way of the sword belongs to us all," Piandao said. "Sokka, continue to train on your own. I know that one day you will become a greater master than I."

Piandao bowed to Sokka and placed the sword back in his hands. Sokka bowed back, his eyes shining. He was a sword master at last!